CPSIA information can be obtained
at www.ICGtesting.com
Printed in the USA
LVIC01n104505121213
364013LV00003B/24

D1210786

Riding on a Beam of Light

By Ramsey Dean
Illustrated by Noah Hamdan

The Light Beam Riders, Ltd.
1555 N. Dearborn Parkway, Suite 14B
Chicago, IL 60610
www.ridingonabeamoflight.com

10 9 8 7 6 5 4 3 2 1

ISBN: 9780989337212

To Lightning Boy, from Weatherman.

"Imagination is more important than knowledge."

- Albert Einstein

The sun had gone down
but deep into the night there burned a light soon to shine so bright.

Young Albert did the most fantastical dreaming -
imagining, wondering, his young mind teeming.
Sometimes he even dreamed about dreaming!

But he did this wide-awake, morning and afternoon, too.
Thinking of ways to make all those dreams come true.

His mother barged in, all this imagination just isn't right.
"Albert, it's past your bedtime.
Turn off that light!"

She kissed his head and said good-night
as she reached for the lamp and turned out the light.
Albert smiled without a peep,
he also liked dreaming in his sleep.

But when the light vanished without a trace,
Albert saw through the darkness as he stared into space.
Here one second, gone the next,
the new mystery of light left Albert perplexed.

Then a thought so exciting popped into his head
that he pulled off the covers and sprang from the bed.
It's not back in the lamp, that much I know.
It shot into the night and out the window.

This thing called light is a magic show -
Where does it come from and where does it go?
Just how fast?
And just how slow?
These are things that I need to know!

He questioned the shadows upon the floor,
this time they revealed something he hadn't seen before.
Light moves forward, against my hand.
It's a force at work... I think I understand!

So if I could make this lamp shine super-bright,
then aim it off into the night,
then flick the switch and hold on tight,
then suddenly I'd be...

Riding on a beam of light!

Out past the clouds, the moon, and then Mars.
Out past the sun, beyond the stars -
the Milky Way no longer in sight.
Oh, how far I could go riding on a beam of light!

I'll have to bring a sweater, it could get cold.

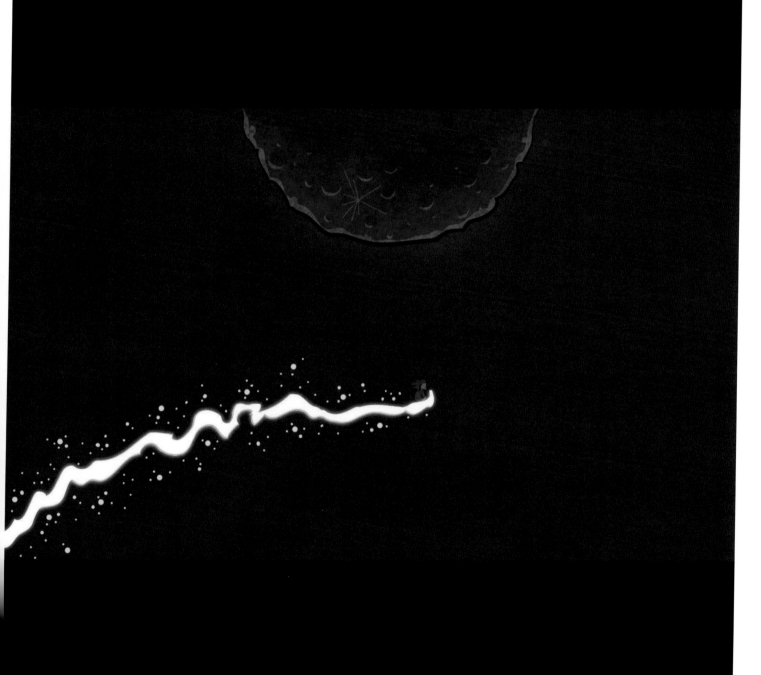

Or have places so hot I'll burn my feet.
Either way, it will be pretty neat!

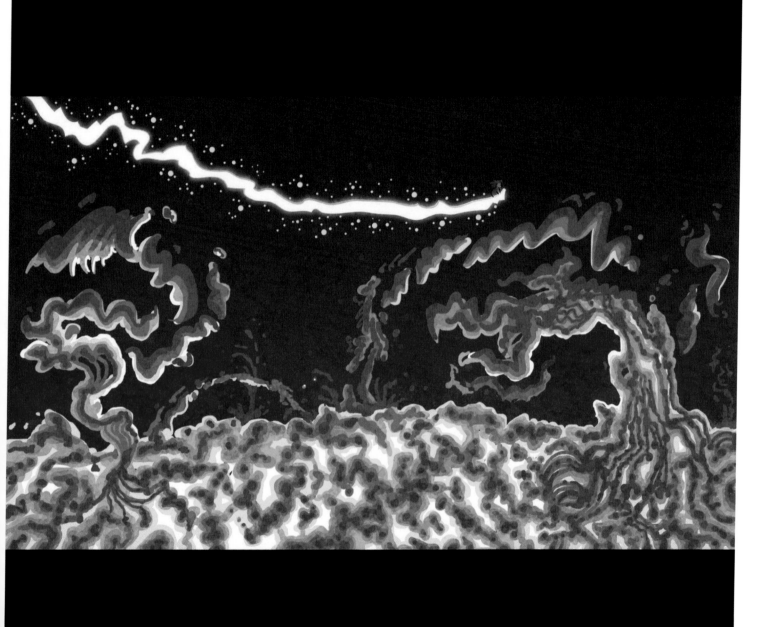

I can see so far when I use my mind,
there's so much to learn, so much to find.
And so much to explore out here in space,
it truly is an amazing pla-

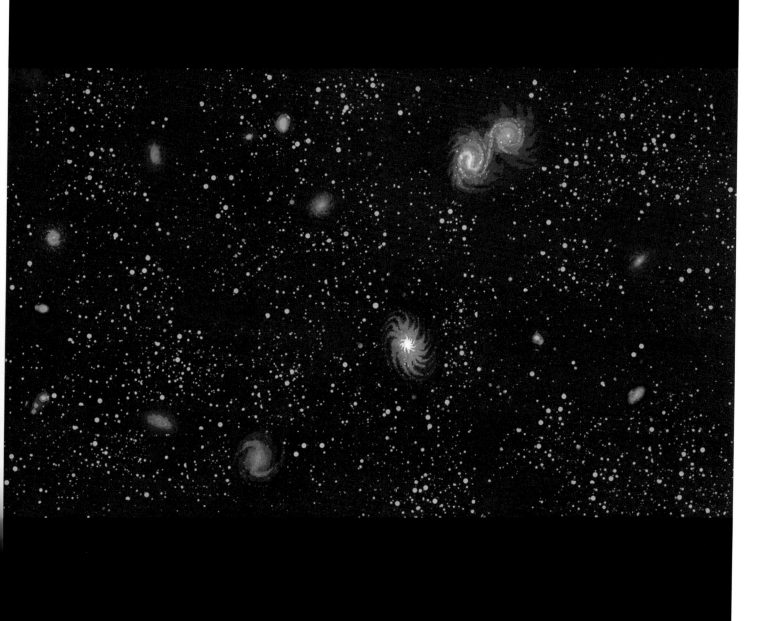

"Albert!"

"I want this lamp to stay off!" his mother said.
"Now you go to sleep, you get in this bed!"

As she tucked him in and again said good-night,
Albert finally spoke and asked, "What is light?"

She puzzled at the question, stumped for an answer.
"It's just light, my dear son, what does it matter?"

"Matter." he thought, as his mother shut the door.
So Albert closed his eyes and imagined some more.

Good Night.

As a boy, Albert Einstein loved to imagine. Whenever his thoughts ran low on ideas, he turned to books to inspire his ever-curious mind. "Logic will get you from A to B, imagination will take you everywhere," he also liked to say. When he mixed the things he'd learn with the things he'd imagine, he discovered a few new ideas that he put in his own books. These books inspired the imaginations of some pretty smart grown-ups and made his mother very proud.

Ramsey Dean is the author of books and screenplays. He was explaining Albert Einstein's use of thought experiments to his son when the two came up with a thought experiment of their own called Riding on a Beam of Light. They live in Chicago, IL.

www.ramseydean.com

Illustrator Noah Hamdan graduated from the Savannah College of Art & Design with a B.F.A. in Visual Effects. He lives in Hopewell, NJ.

www.noahhamdan.com

The LIght Beam Riders
1555 N. Dearborn Parkway, Suite 14B
Chicago, IL 60610
www.ridingonabeamoflight.com

Text copyright 2012,2013 Ramsey Dean
Illustrations copyright 2013 Noah Hamdan

Riding on a Beam of Light, First Edition

All Rights Reserved.

ISBN: 9780989337212

10 9 8 7 6 5 4 3 2 1